W9-AVO-995

This

Moshi Moshi Kawaii

book belongs to

....

....

Ruffle Moshi

Ruffle Moshi's Friends

My dress has three frills.

Polka Dot Moshi

Polka Dot Moshi's Friends

My outfit has white polka dots.

Lovely Moshi

Lovely Moshi's Friends

My outfit is covered in little hearts.

Aloha Panda

Aloha Panda's Friends

My costume has blue flowers on it.

Shop Assistant Moshi

Shop Assistant Moshi's Friends

I wear a ribbon around my neck.

Mermaid Moshi

Mermaid Moshi's Friends

I wear a shell bikini.

Moshi Moshi Kawaii®

Meet the Moshi
and all their friends!

Strawberry Moshi

Strawberry Moshi's Friends

I wear a strawberry outfit and become Strawberry Princess Moshi when I dress up.

Strawberry Princess Moshi

Strawberry Princess Moshi's Friends

I wear a strawberry-patterned dress and a ribbon.

Cinderella Moshi

Cinderella Moshi's Friends

I wear a sparkly blue dress.

Snow White Moshi

Snow White Moshi's Friends

I wear a ribbon and carry a red apple.

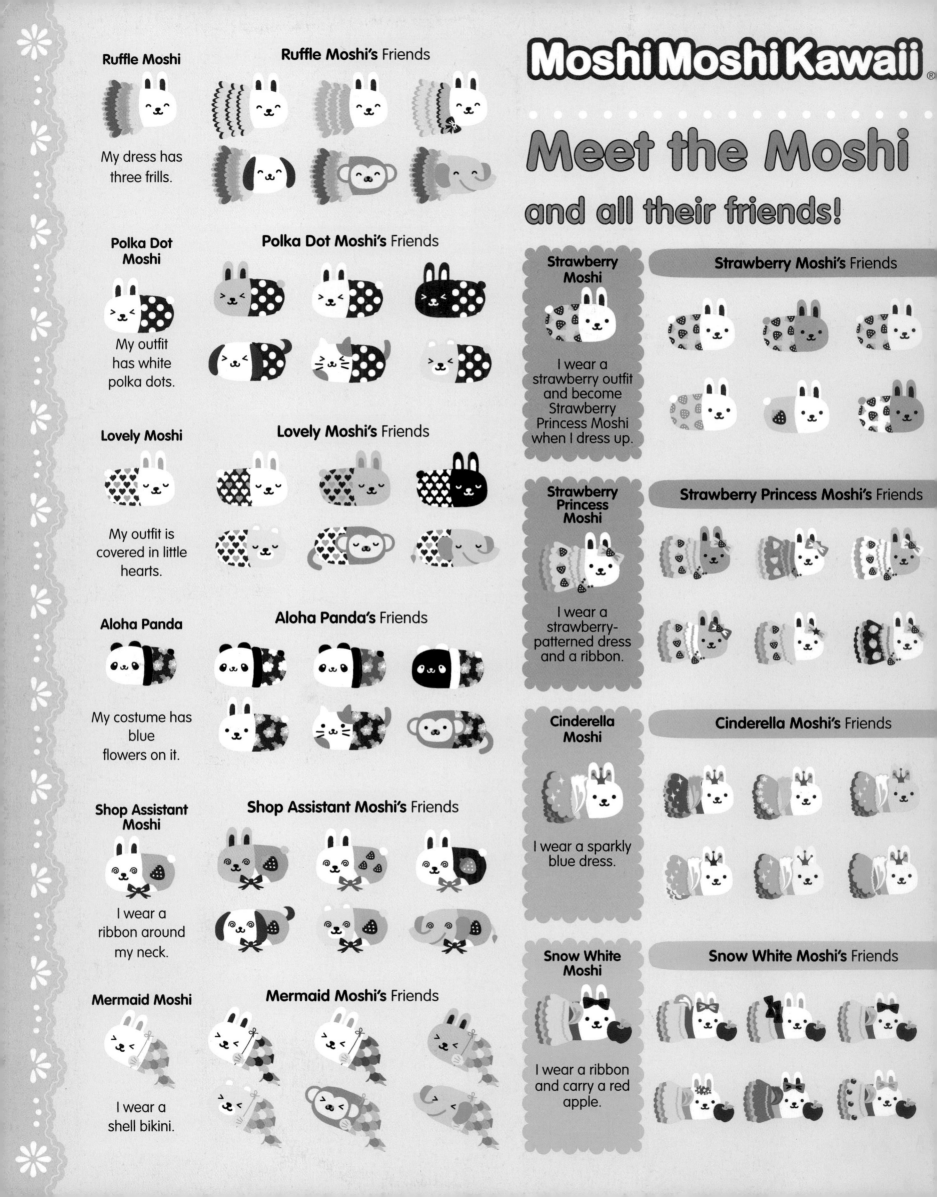

At first glance, each Moshi looks the same. Look again and you'll see they're all different. Find each type in the book.

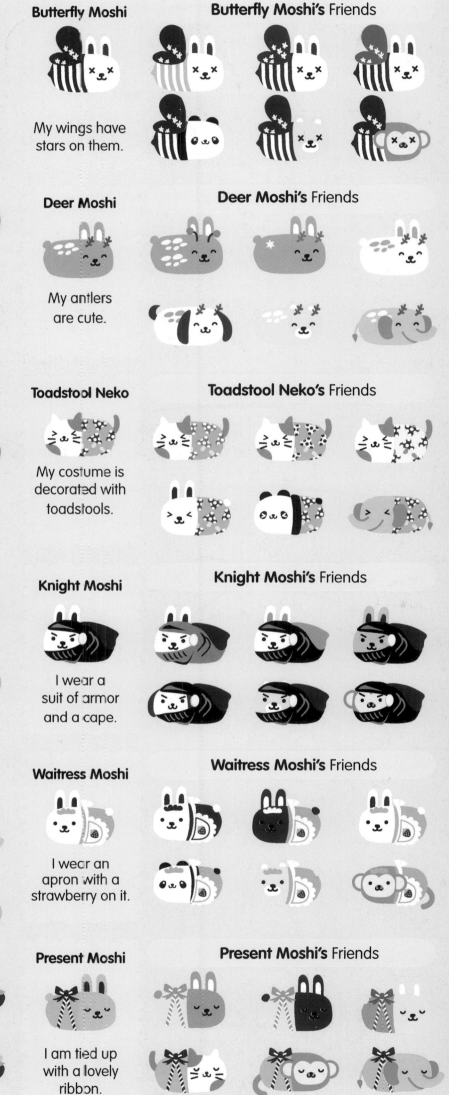

Butterfly Moshi

My wings have stars on them.

Butterfly Moshi's Friends

Deer Moshi

My antlers are cute.

Deer Moshi's Friends

Toadstool Neko

My costume is decorated with toadstools.

Toadstool Neko's Friends

Knight Moshi

I wear a suit of armor and a cape.

Knight Moshi's Friends

Waitress Moshi

I wear an apron with a strawberry on it.

Waitress Moshi's Friends

Present Moshi

I am tied up with a lovely ribbon.

Present Moshi's Friends

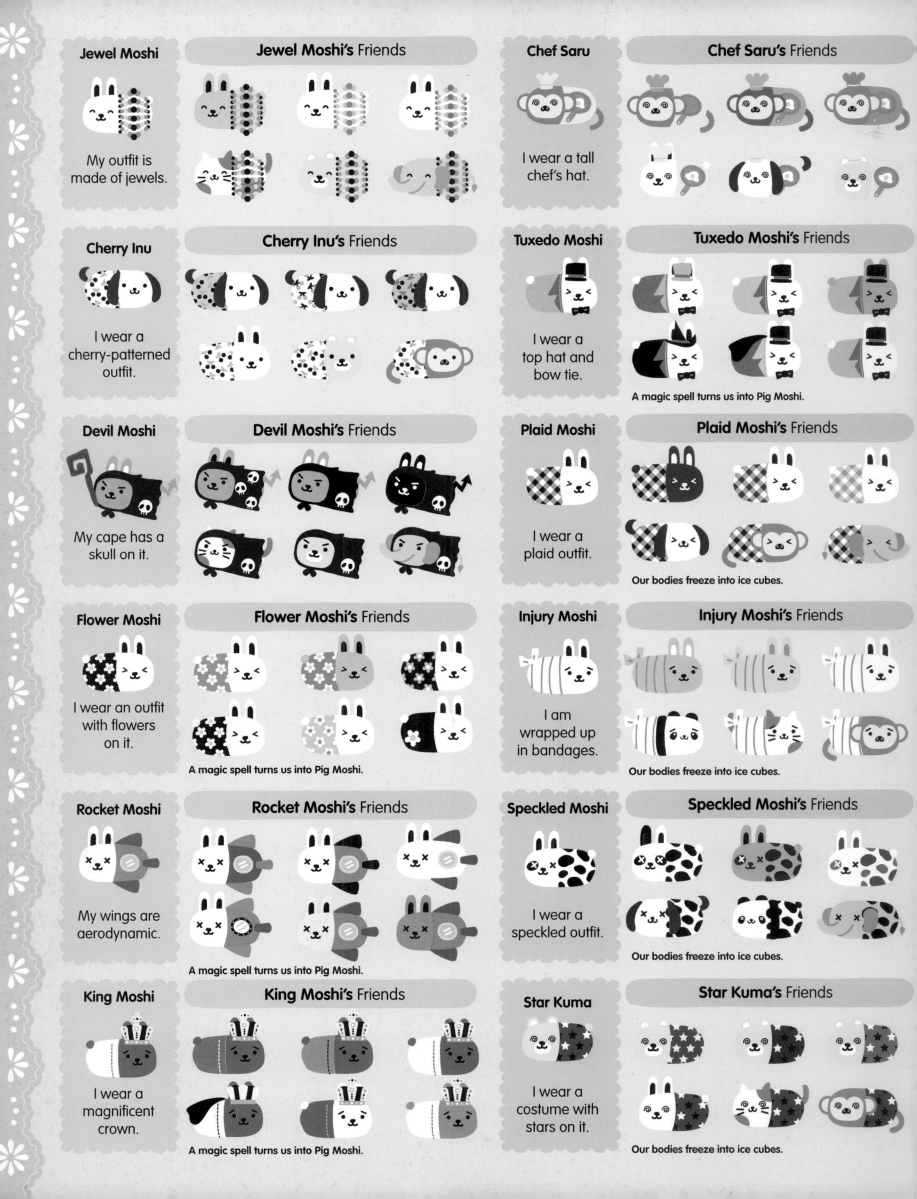

Jewel Moshi

My outfit is made of jewels.

Jewel Moshi's Friends

Chef Saru

I wear a tall chef's hat.

Chef Saru's Friends

Cherry Inu

I wear a cherry-patterned outfit.

Cherry Inu's Friends

Tuxedo Moshi

I wear a top hat and bow tie.

Tuxedo Moshi's Friends

A magic spell turns us into Pig Moshi.

Devil Moshi

My cape has a skull on it.

Devil Moshi's Friends

Plaid Moshi

I wear a plaid outfit.

Plaid Moshi's Friends

Our bodies freeze into ice cubes.

Flower Moshi

I wear an outfit with flowers on it.

Flower Moshi's Friends

A magic spell turns us into Pig Moshi.

Injury Moshi

I am wrapped up in bandages.

Injury Moshi's Friends

Our bodies freeze into ice cubes.

Rocket Moshi

My wings are aerodynamic.

Rocket Moshi's Friends

A magic spell turns us into Pig Moshi.

Speckled Moshi

I wear a speckled outfit.

Speckled Moshi's Friends

Our bodies freeze into ice cubes.

King Moshi

I wear a magnificent crown.

King Moshi's Friends

A magic spell turns us into Pig Moshi.

Star Kuma

I wear a costume with stars on it.

Star Kuma's Friends

Our bodies freeze into ice cubes.

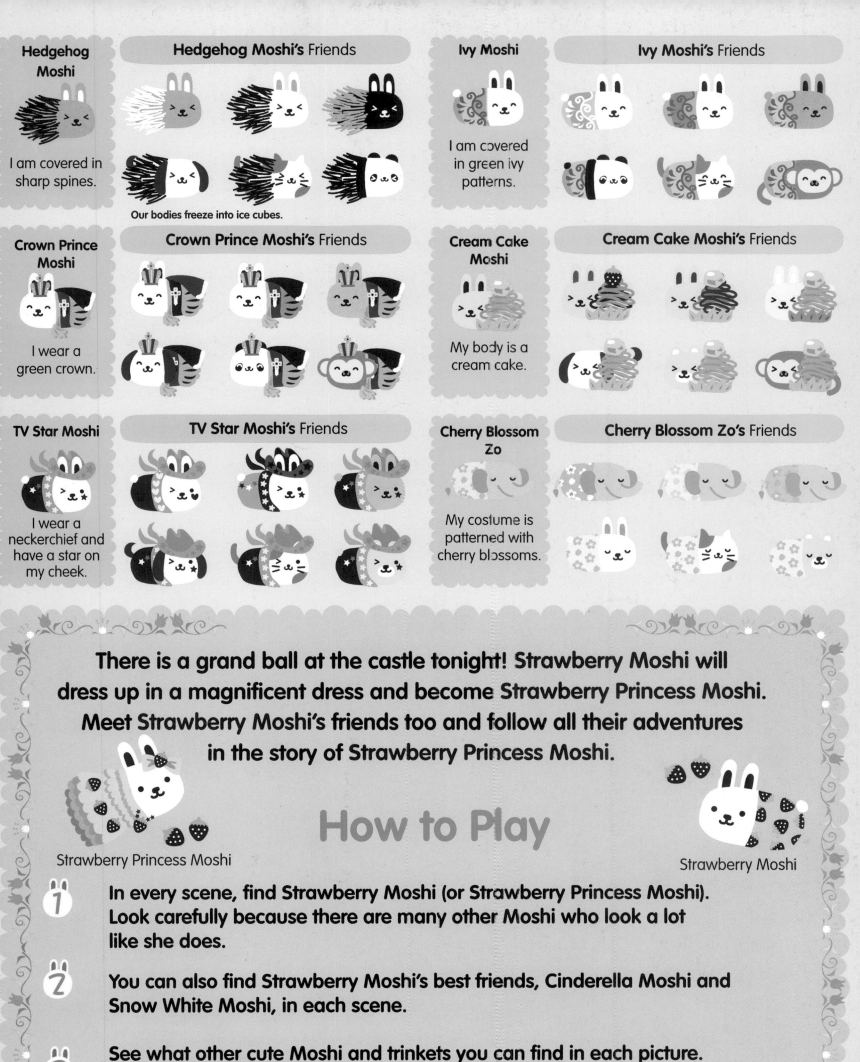

Hedgehog Moshi

I am covered in sharp spines.

Hedgehog Moshi's Friends

Our bodies freeze into ice cubes.

Ivy Moshi

I am covered in green ivy patterns.

Ivy Moshi's Friends

Crown Prince Moshi

I wear a green crown.

Crown Prince Moshi's Friends

Cream Cake Moshi

My body is a cream cake.

Cream Cake Moshi's Friends

TV Star Moshi

I wear a neckerchief and have a star on my cheek.

TV Star Moshi's Friends

Cherry Blossom Zo

My costume is patterned with cherry blossoms.

Cherry Blossom Zo's Friends

There is a grand ball at the castle tonight! Strawberry Moshi will dress up in a magnificent dress and become Strawberry Princess Moshi. Meet Strawberry Moshi's friends too and follow all their adventures in the story of Strawberry Princess Moshi.

Strawberry Princess Moshi

Strawberry Moshi

How to Play

1 In every scene, find Strawberry Moshi (or Strawberry Princess Moshi). Look carefully because there are many other Moshi who look a lot like she does.

2 You can also find Strawberry Moshi's best friends, Cinderella Moshi and Snow White Moshi, in each scene.

3 See what other cute Moshi and trinkets you can find in each picture. Which is your favorite?

Cinderella's Town

Crown Prince Moshi is throwing a grand ball tonight. **Strawberry Moshi** has come to meet her friends and find a dress to wear.

Where is **Strawberry Moshi**?

Where is **Cinderella Moshi**?

Where is **Snow White Moshi**?

Strawberry Boutique

Strawberry Moshi has come to the **Strawberry Boutique** to find the perfect strawberry dress.

Where is **Strawberry Moshi?**

Where is **Cinderella Moshi?**

Where is **Snow White Moshi?**

Where are these Moshi?

Ruffle Moshi, you are chatting.

Are you with your sweetheart, **Polka Dot Moshi?**

Lovely Moshi, you are keeping a straight face.

Aloha Panda, have you found your favorite dress?

Shop Assistant Moshi, you look very busy.

1

Someone has lost her purse. Can you find it?

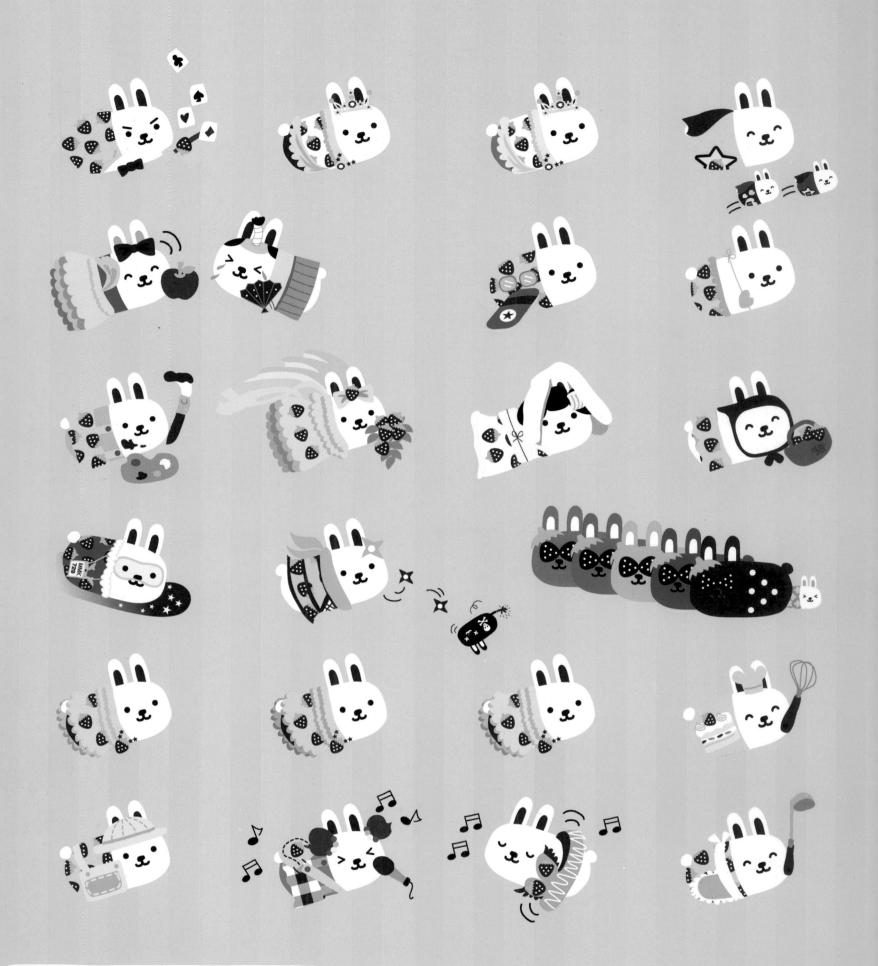

The Changing Room

Strawberry Moshi has finally chosen the dress to turn her into **Strawberry Princess Moshi**.

Where is **Strawberry Princess Moshi**?

Where is **Cinderella Moshi**?

Where is **Snow White Moshi**?

Where are these Moshi?

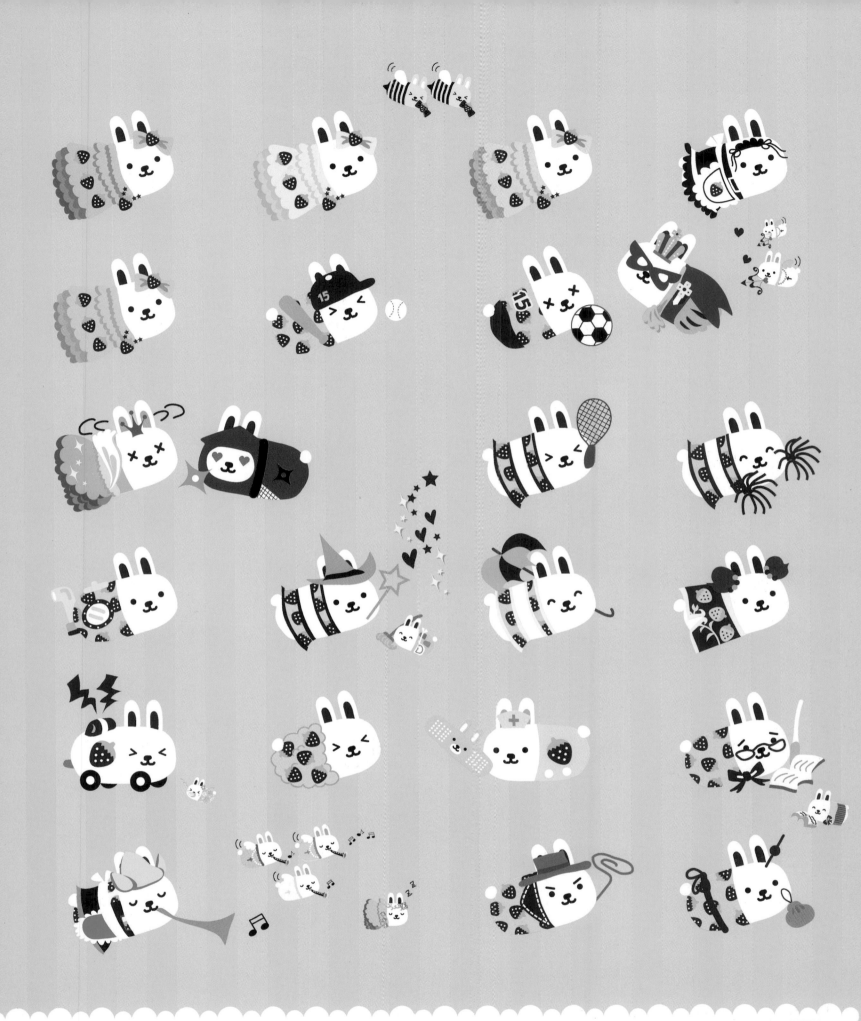

Strawberry Nurse Moshi

Strawberry Red Riding Hood Moshi

Strawberry Witch Moshi

Strawberry Ninja Moshi

Strawberry Ambulance Moshi

To The Castle

It's time for the ball! Everyone is heading to **Crown Prince Moshi's** castle.

Where is **Strawberry Princess Moshi**?

Where is **Cinderella Moshi**?

Where is **Snow White Moshi**?

Where are these Moshi?

Are you taking a rest, **Mermaid Moshi**?

Butterfly Moshi, look out!

Enjoy your picnic, **Deer Moshi**.

Toadstool Neko, those mushrooms look good.

Knight Moshi, you are welcoming the guests!

2 There are two balls in the picture. Can you find them?

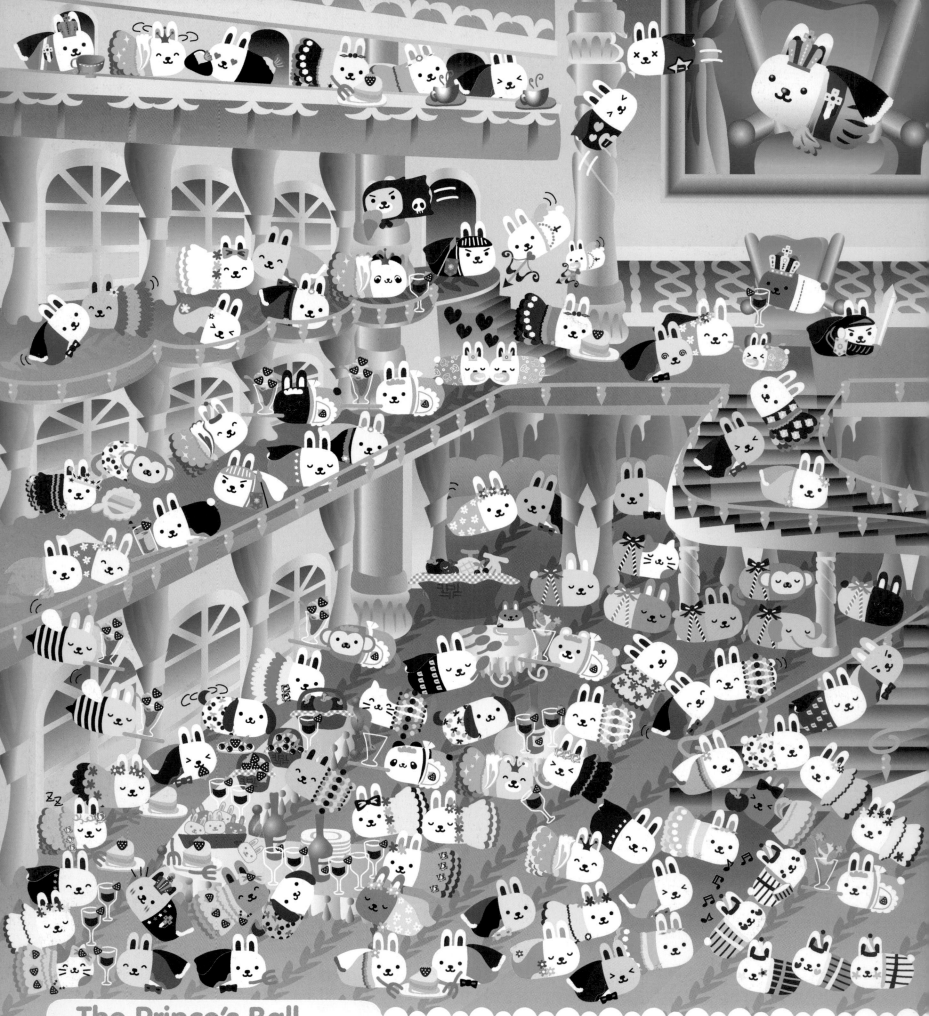

The Prince's Ball

At the castle, the ball has started and everyone is having fun.

Where is **Strawberry Princess Moshi**?

Where is Cinderella Moshi?

Where is **Snow White Moshi**?

Where are these Moshi?

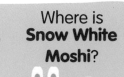

Hurry up, **Waitress Moshi**.

Present Moshi, you are enchanting.

Jewel Moshi, you dance so well.

Cherry Inu, you are enjoying the food.

Devil Moshi, you are casting a magic spell!

3 There are three mirrors in the picture. Can you find them?

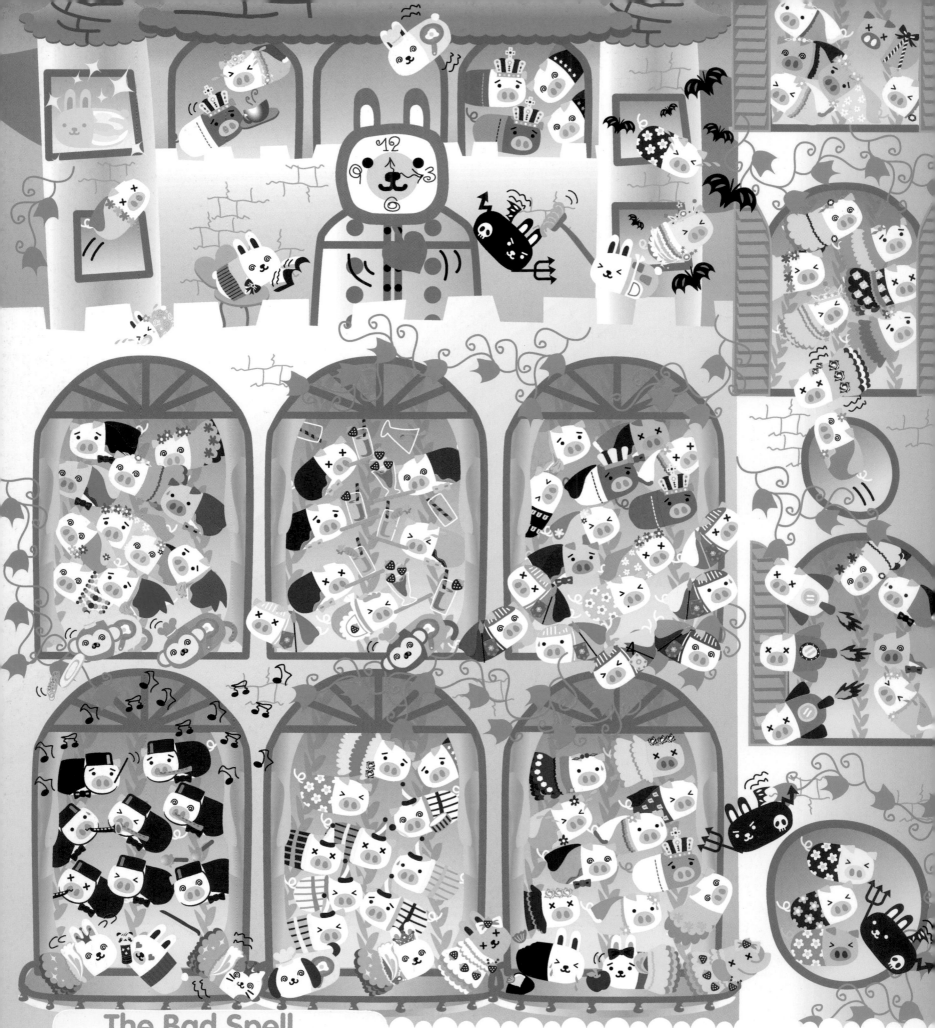

The Bad Spell

Oh, no! **Devil Moshi's** magic spell has turned some Moshi into pigs. Has **Strawberry Princess Moshi** escaped?

Where is **Strawberry Princess Moshi**?

Where is **Cinderella Moshi**?

Where is **Snow White Moshi**?

Where are these Moshi?

Don't cry, **Flower Pig Moshi**.

Rocket Pig Moshi, you can fly away.

King Pig Moshi, you are very kind.

Chef Saru, you have dropped your food.

Call for help, **Tuxedo Pig Moshi**!

4 There are four cups in the picture. Can you find them?

START

The Secret Maze

Strawberry Princess Moshi has found the passageway to the **Devil Moshi Cave**. Help the Moshi through the maze to break the magic spell.

Follow a path through the maze with your finger. Look out for dead ends!

FINISH

Devil Moshi Cave

It's so cold inside the **Devil Moshi Cave** that the Moshi have turned into ice cubes. Is **Strawberry Princess Moshi** all right?

Where is **Strawberry Princess Moshi**?

Where is **Cinderella Moshi**?

Where is **Snow White Moshi**?

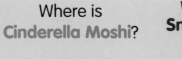

Where are these Moshi?

Plaid Moshi, who have you bumped into?

What are you writing, **Injury Moshi?**

Speckled Moshi, look out for the **Devil Moshi.**

Wave your flag, **Star Kuma.**

Enjoy the slide, **Hedgehog Moshi.**

5 There are five bats flying in the picture. Can you find them?

The Shadow Game

Devil Moshi gives **Strawberry Princess Moshi** a challenge.

The spell will be broken if she can find each of these Moshi's shadows. Can you help her?

Which shadow belongs to **Flute Player Moshi**?

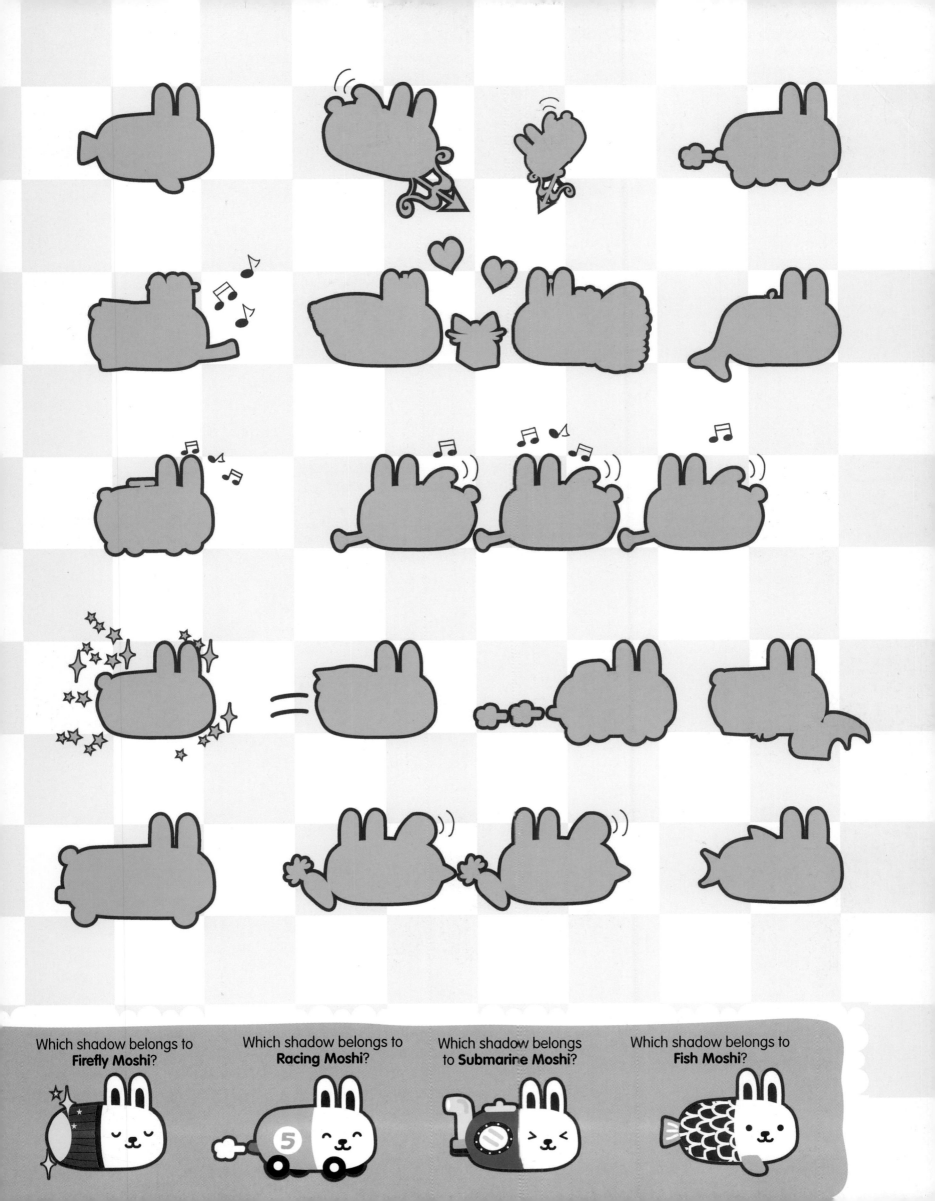

Which shadow belongs to **Firefly Moshi**?

Which shadow belongs to **Racing Moshi**?

Which shadow belongs to **Submarine Moshi**?

Which shadow belongs to **Fish Moshi**?

The Big Celebration

Strawberry Princess Moshi has broken the spell! There is a big party to celebrate. Will **Strawberry Princess Moshi** meet her sweetheart, **Crown Prince Moshi**?

Where is **Strawberry Princess Moshi**?

Where is **Crown Prince Moshi**?

Where is **Cinderella Moshi**?

Where is **Snow White Moshi**?

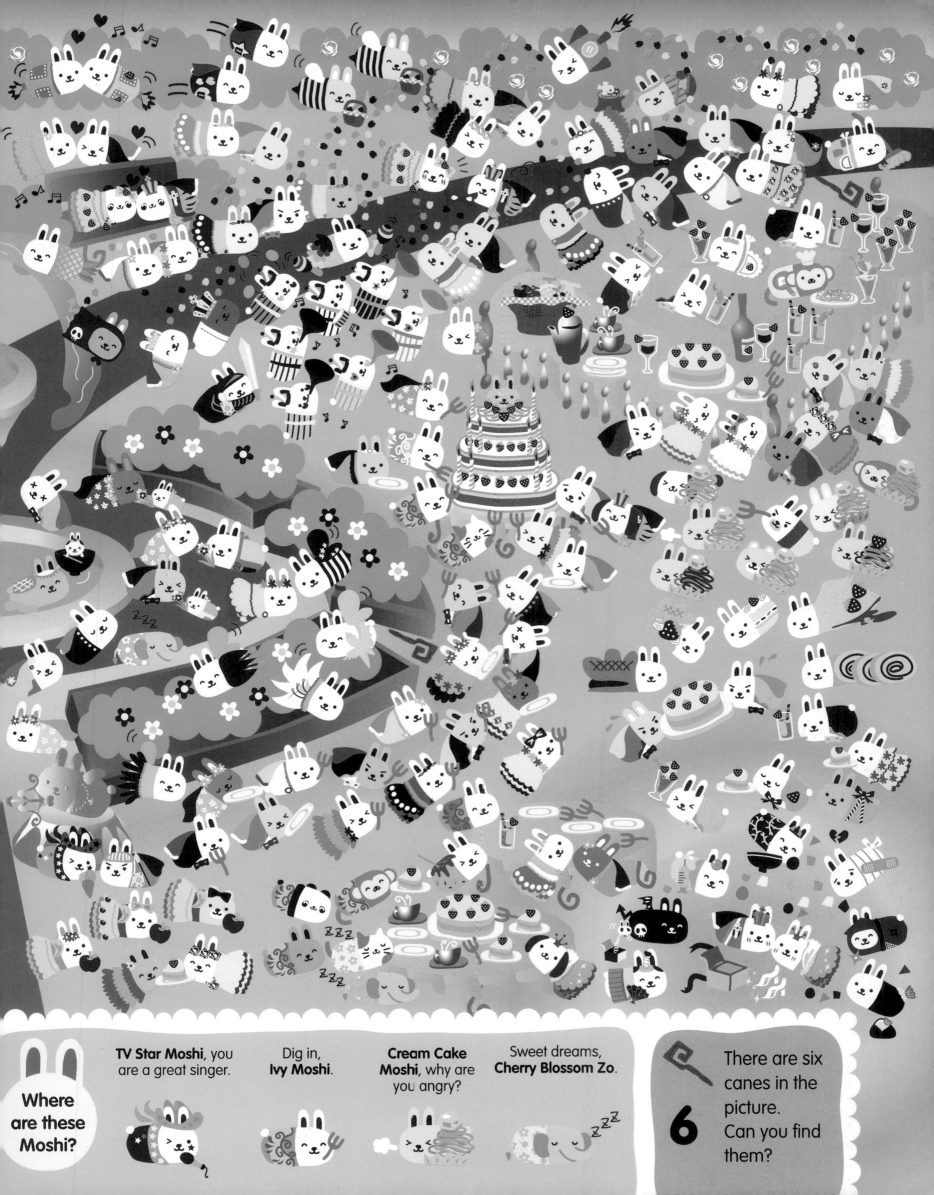

Where are these Moshi?

TV Star Moshi, you are a great singer.

Dig in, **Ivy Moshi**.

Cream Cake Moshi, why are you angry?

Sweet dreams, **Cherry Blossom Zo**.

6 There are six canes in the picture. Can you find them?

The Flower Wedding

Moshi Love Stories

Follow the love stories of Strawberry Princess Moshi and her friends, from Cinderella's Town to The Flower Wedding.

Strawberry Princess Moshi

Cinderella's Town

A masked Moshi is looking at Strawberry Moshi.

Strawberry Boutique

He is also watching her in the boutique.

The Changing Room

Who is this mysterious Moshi?

To The Castle

He is still watching her . . .

The Prince's Ball

even when he dances with other Moshi.

The Bad Spell

The masked Moshi helps her when she's in danger.

The Secret Maze

And he is always right behind her.

Devil Moshi Cave

Who could this Moshi be?

The Shadow Game

Where has this mask come from?

The Big Celebration

The masked Moshi was Crown Prince Moshi!

The Flower Wedding

Three cheers!

Crown Prince Moshi asks Strawberry Princess Moshi to marry him. It's the best day of Strawberry Princess Moshi's life!

Cinderella's Town

Cinderella Moshi has many admirers who offer her gifts. But she turns down Injury Moshi when he offers her a bandage.

Cinderella Moshi

Strawberry Boutique

She also refuses the fan that Tono-sama Moshi gives her.

The Changing Room

She turns down the star that Ninja Moshi wants to give her.

To The Castle

She doesn't want Silk Moshi's noodles.

The Prince's Ball

She turns down Tenmusu Moshi's gift.

The Bad Spell

She says no when Oyaji Moshi tries to give her a doll.

The Secret Maze

She does not want a jack-in-the-box either.

Devil Moshi Cave

She certainly does not want Doctor Moshi's syringe.

The Shadow Game

Somebody is offering her a box . . .

The Big Celebration

inside is a pair of beautiful glass slippers!

The Flower Wedding

Cinderella Moshi loves the glass slippers and lives happily ever after with her Prince Moshi.

Cinderella's Town

Kind **Snow White Moshi** gives an apple to anyone who needs cheering up, like Baby Moshi.

Snow White Moshi

Strawberry Boutique

She makes Injury Moshi feel better.

The Changing Room

She comforts Tono-sama Moshi.

To The Castle

She wishes Ninja Moshi good luck.

The Prince's Ball

She tells Silk Moshi not to cry.

The Bad Spell

She wipes away Tenmusu Moshi's tears.

The Secret Maze

She accepts the apple Evil Witch Moshi gives her.

Devil Moshi Cave

She takes a bite and falls into a deep sleep.

The Shadow Game

Snow White Moshi wi l not wake up.

The Big Celebration

A prince wakes her with a kiss.

The Flower Wedding

The two marry and live happily ever after.

Keep on searching!

Here are even more Moshi to find.
Look again at each scene and see if
you can spot them.

Moshi in every scene

Find these Moshi in all the scenes from Cinderella's Town to the Flower Wedding.

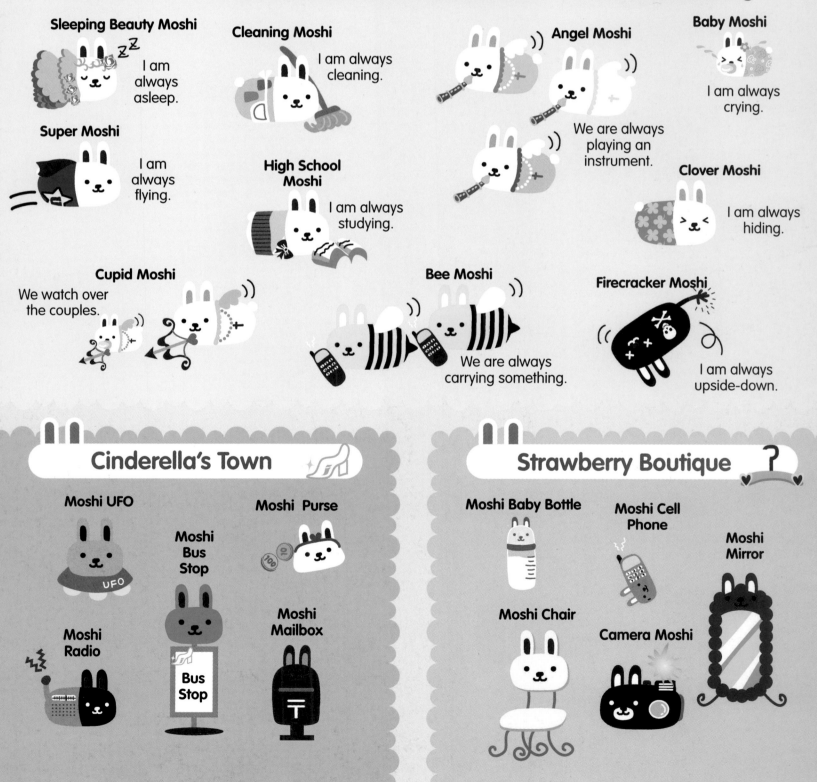

Sleeping Beauty Moshi
I am always asleep.

Cleaning Moshi
I am always cleaning.

Angel Moshi
We are always playing an instrument.

Baby Moshi
I am always crying.

Super Moshi
I am always flying.

High School Moshi
I am always studying.

Clover Moshi
I am always hiding.

Cupid Moshi
We watch over the couples.

Bee Moshi
We are always carrying something.

Firecracker Moshi
I am always upside-down.

Cinderella's Town

Moshi UFO

Moshi Purse

Moshi Bus Stop

Bus Stop

Moshi Radio

Moshi Mailbox

Strawberry Boutique

Moshi Baby Bottle

Moshi Cell Phone

Moshi Mirror

Moshi Chair

Camera Moshi

To The Castle

Moshi Onigiri

Moshi Plant

Moshi Balloon

Moshi Hot Air Balloon

Moshi Battery Charger

BATTERY CHARGER

Devil Moshi Cave

Moshi Syringe

Pirate Moshi

Moshi Shaved Ice

Moshi Fish Bone

Moshi Poop

The Prince's Ball

Moshi Cookies

Moshi Cello

Moshi Dessert

Moshi Banjo

Moshi Harp

The Big Celebration

Takoyaki Moshi

Pineapple Moshi

Watermelon Moshi

Strawberry Cream Puff Moshi

Cake Moshi

The Bad Spell

Moshi Bench

Treasure Moshi

Moshi Christmas Tree

Moshi Clock

Moshi Parachute

Copyright © 2003 by Mind Wave Inc.
All rights reserved.
MoshiMoshiKawaii ® is a registered trademark
Original Japanese edition published by GAKKEN Co. Ltd.
Original title: USACOLLE FRIENDS, ICHIGO-HIME WO SAGASE!
This edition published by arrangement with
Gakken Education Publishing Co. Ltd., Tokyo, Japan, through PLUS LICENS AB.
First U.S. edition 2011
Library of Congress Cataloging-in-Publication Data is available.
Library of Congress Catalog Card Number 2010042842
ISBN 978-0-7636-5203-6
11 12 13 14 15 16 CCP 10 9 8 7 6 5 4 3 2 1
Printed in Shenzhen, Guangdong, China
This book was typeset in VAG Rounded.
The illustrations were produced digitally.
Candlewick Press, 99 Dover Street, Somerville, Massachusetts 02144
visit us at www.candlewick.com
www.moshimoshikawaii.com

C | P

CANDLEWICK PRESS
www.candlewick.com

Keep on searching for Strawberry Moshi in